Paul, David, Brian and Roger are parents as well
as poets, so they definitely know the truth about
parents. Whether this collection tells the whole truth
is up to you to decide – maybe they've left the really
embarrassing bits out! If you'd like them to visit your
school and tell you the truth about parents (as well as
the truth about teachers), they can.

David Parkins has illustrated numerous books, ranging
from maths textbooks to the *Beano*. His picture books
have been shortlisted for the Smarties Book Prize and
the Kurt Maschler Award. He lives in Canada with his
wife, three children and six cats.

The TRUTH about PARENTS

Hilarious Rhymes by
Paul Cookson, David Harmer
Brian Moses and Roger Stevens

Illustrated by
David Parkins

To Sam

All true – of course!

MACMILLAN CHILDREN'S BOOKS

*For John Foster – a pioneer in children's poetry,
to whom we owe a special debt of gratitude.
Thanks for paving the way for the rest of us!*

First published 2009 by Macmillan Children's Books

This edition published 2013 by Macmillan Children's Books
a division of Macmillan Publishers Limited
20 New Wharf Road, London N1 9RR
Basingstoke and Oxford
Associated companies throughout the world
www.panmacmillan.com

ISBN 978-1-4472-4212-3

Text copyright © Paul Cookson, David Harmer, Brian Moses and
Roger Stevens 2009
Illustrations copyright © David Parkins 2009

The right of Paul Cookson, David Harmer, Brian Moses, Roger Stevens and David
Parkins to be identified as the authors and illustrator of this work has been asserted
by them in accordance with the Copyright, Designs and Patents Act 1988.

1 3 5 7 9 8 6 4 2

A CIP catalogue record for this book is available from
the British Library.

Printed and bound by CPI Group (UK) Ltd, Croydon CR0 4YY

Contents

My Family and Me

Dad is like a hippo
with a great big yawn
Mum is like a lion
lying out on the lawn
My sister's like a monkey
hanging from a tree
But I am like a wise old owl
as brainy as can be

Roger Stevens

When Mum Giggles

I like it when Mum's happy
It's the best sound in the world
She goes all red and snorts and laughs
Looks like her childhood photographs
She wriggles and she giggles just like a little girl

Her nose it starts to twitch
And her lips begin to curl
Her eyes begin to twinkle
And her dimples start to wrinkle
She wriggles and she giggles just like a little girl

Her worries seem to fade away
And all the years unfurl
She's innocence and beauty when
To prove the truth of youth again
She wriggles and she giggles just like a little girl

Paul Cookson

My Dad's a Stuntman

Some Dads work on buses
others work on trains
or pound the beat with great flat feet
or mend and clean the drains.

Some Dads dig with shovels
others sail the sea
some are cooks or publish books
have chat shows on TV.

But my dad
jumps off the top of a giant skyscraper, lands
THUMP on a car roof, rolls over and leaps
through a stack of blazing tyres, dives
on to a motorbike and roars up the road.

Some Dads sing in choirs
others play guitars
some have naps or gaze at maps
of planets, moons and stars.

Some Dads play at football
others like to draw
some relax with books of facts
or paint the kitchen door.

But my dad
sleeps curled up on a bed of rusty nails, swims
across an icy pool a hundred times before breakfast
sets fire to himself and falls out of a plane
all in a day's work to my dad.

David Harmer

Exits

Our mum is so theatrical.
When she leaves our house
she takes one encore after another.

'Bye, Mum,' we say
as she exits.

And then we stay
exactly where we are
and wait
for one, perhaps two minutes
till there's a ratatat-tat
on the door.

And when we open it
there's Mum,
handbag wide open
stirring the contents
till she says,
'I can't find my keys.'

And in she'll come
then out again
with the keys in her hand.

And then we stay
exactly where we are
and wait
for one, perhaps two minutes
till there's a key in the lock
and this time it's,
'Oh, I forgot,
there's a cake in the cupboard
if you're hungry . . .'

Our mum is so theatrical,
her encores
mathematical,
two at least,
sometimes more
before she's finally
out the door
and away.

Brian Moses

My Mother Is

My mother is a diamond
An emerald
A pearl

A sapphire
A ruby
She's that kind of a girl

An amethyst
A moonstone
A lapis lazuli

My mother rocks!
Yes, she's a gem
And quite precious to me

Roger Stevens

Mum & Dad

Tenderskin & Roughchin

Dawngreeter & Toastjuggler

Cuddlebear & Grizzlybear

Firmhand & Strongarm

Sadsmile & Grinner

Busybee & Grasshopper

Spicegrinder & Potstirrer

Sunsoaker & Ballspinner

Spidershrieker & Jarcatcher

Taleteller & Dreamweaver

Earthmother & Earthmover

Roger Stevens

They Don't Know Everything

My mum and stepdad
Know everything
Or so they think
But

Only I know
The routes of alien spaceships
Criss-crossing the night sky

Only I know
The hidden art of invisibility
And how to fly

Only I know
The password in the hidden door
Behind the rakes in the garden shed

Only I know the secret tongue of lizards
And why the dragons
Are all dead

I'll never tell my parents what I've found
And when I'm grown I'll keep these secrets
Safe and sound

Roger Stevens

My Dad

My dad's a cobbler.
He mends shoes.
He's my cobbling dad.

He dropped the hammer on his toe.
He's my hobbling, cobbling dad.

Dad had an argument with a customer.
He's my squabbling, hobbling, cobbling dad.

So he made her a raspberry jelly.
He's my wobbling, squabbling, hobbling, cobbling dad.

Then he ate it all himself.
He's my gobbling, wobbling, squabbling, hobbling,
cobbling dad.

Roger Stevens

THWACK
WHACK!

Superman's Sister

Our mum must be Superman's sister,
we're amazed at what she does . . .

Fighting monstrous piles of washing,
battling the bulky duvets,
taming the horror that's our Hoover,
rescuing us from those terrifying spiders,
wrestling the dog who never wants to be brushed,
finding big bunny who's always on the run,

and . . .
dashing at streak-of-lightning speed
to save us all from being late for school!

Brian Moses

The World's Greatest Goalie

I fly down the wing
Make a thunderous shot
Score a fabulous goal
That's the tenth I've got
I love my mum
I love her a lot
Is she a great goalie?
No, she's not

Roger Stevens

My Mum's Put Me on the Transfer List

On offer:
one nippy striker, eight years old
has scored seven goals this season
has nifty footwork and a big smile
knows how to dive in the penalty box
can get filthy and muddy within two minutes
guaranteed to wreck his kit each week.
This is a FREE TRANSFER
but he comes with running expenses
weeks of washing shirts and shorts
socks and vests, a pair of trainers
needs to scoff huge amounts
of chips and burgers, beans and apples
pop and cola, crisps and oranges
endless packs of chewing gum.
This offer open until the end of the season
I'll have him back then
at least until the cricket starts.
Any takers?

David Harmer

When Mum Takes Me FootBall Training

Mum gets out her old bike and pedals like crazy
she makes me run to the park
I get red-faced and breathless.
When we arrive we play one against one
she picks up the football and kicks it hard
as high as a bird in the big blue sky
it floats up there like a lost balloon
comes thundering down and I say to myself,
'Do I dare head it? Do I? Yes!'
But I don't and I miss it, nearly fall over
and head it back on the fourth bounce
better still trap it, twist past three defenders
and run like a dart for the penalty spot
draw back my foot and belt it for goal.
My mum does her arms-stretched, starfish-shaped
leap-like-a-cat save, tips it just round the post
and we sit and laugh, then buy an ice cream
take our time going home.

David Harmer

When Dad Took Me Football Training

He put on his new trainers
he put on his new jogging bottoms
he put his fancy new football
in the car with the dog.

We drove to the park
I got out and went in goal
I stood there for ages.

Dad kicked the ball
the dog brought it back
Dad side-footed the ball
the dog pushed it back
Dad toe-poked the ball
the dog shoved it back
Dad tapped the ball
the dog rolled it back.

The sun came out. The dog rolled over.
Day lay on the grass and went to sleep.

I flicked the ball on to my right foot with my left
kept it off the ground for twenty-five keepy-uppies
dropped it from my chest to my knee to my foot
I booted the ball into Dad's back.

He grunted
the dog barked down his ear
so we all got into the car
and Dad drove us home.

David Harmer

Dazzling Derek

That's my dad shouting at me
from the touchline
like he does every game we play.

I don't know why
I think we do quite well really
this week we're only losing ten—one
and I've scored three times
twice in my goal
and once in theirs

not bad for a goalie.

Last week I was on the wing
it was brilliant
I nearly scored a million times
we still lost
but who was counting?

My dad was
he got really angry
there's no pleasing him.

What he really wants to do
is to shrink back to being ten like me
slip on to the field
score the winning goal
with seconds to go
defeat staring us in the face
Dazzling Derek saves the day!

But he can't
so he jumps up and down on the touchline
shouts at me
mutters and kicks the grass
stubs his toe and yells
nearly gets sent off the field by the ref

where's the fun in that?

David Harmer

Pear-shaped Haiku

Mum and Dad both say

That things have gone all pear-shaped

And for them, they have

Paul Cookson

Reading Habits

When Mum reads
Her eyes are wide
Her eyebrows raised in anticipation
And her lips are pursed eternally
As she licks her fingers
To quickly turn the pages

When Dad reads
He blinks and focuses
Furrows his brow
Yawns and scratches inside his ears
His tongue peeping out of his mouth
Then dribbles as his eyes droop and his head nods
And the book lies open on his chest
While he snores in his favourite chair

Paul Cookson

Mum's Mouthfuls

We all know Mum's mouthfuls!

If she wants us to eat something up
She says, 'Go on, have another mouthful.'
Then she ladles out
Enough to make a hippopotamus choke
Cabbage, salad, peas, parsnips –
All the grotty stuff
That we normally leave on the plate.
'It's good for you,' she says.
'Have another mouthful . . .'

It's always the same.
Mum's idea of what we can cram
Into our mouths is way out of line.
'Muesli is good for you,' she says.
'Have another mouthful.'
And half the packet appears in the dish.

And then, of course,
When we start to complain, she says,
'Don't talk with your mouth full . . .'

But we get our own back . . .
For when Mum's trying to slim
And she says, 'I'll just have a
Tiny piece more of that delicious cake.'
We break off a huge slab
And when she complains, we say,
'Mum, it's only a mouthful!'

Brian Moses

Dad's Got a Ukulele

Dad's got a ukulele
He's ukulele mad
He plays and plays it daily
My ukulele dad

He's ukulele bonkers
He's happy and he's glad
My grinning, humming, finger-strumming
Ukulele dad

Paul Cookson

Rinky tinky tinky diddly dink!

Wait and see . . .

Dad was a 'wait and see' man.
Decisions took days to arrive.
I knew I'd get nowhere
if I needled and whined.
He'd take his time and then maybe,
when all the heavenly bodies had realigned
and the time was right,
he'd say what he'd decided:
'Yes, you can' or 'No, you can't'.

With some dads, 'wait and see'
meant you'd probably be OK,
get what you wanted, give it time.
Not mine. He'd need working on
by Mum, she'd get round him,
make him think it was his idea
all along.

She knew what he was like,
he'd been slow to decide all his life –
new house, new carpets, new furniture,
new stereo system – 'Let's sleep on it,'
he'd say, as if in the night
some visitation would appear
and give a sign, so in the morning
he'd know which decision was right.

Dad was always a 'wait and see' man
and sometimes it seemed an eternity,
all those times I waited and saw
whether what Dad finally decided
was what I was hoping for . . .

Brian Moses

My Birthday Barbecue

There's a queue at the barbecue
Dad is telling a tale or two.

Playing football with George Best
Batting with Botham at the Test
A guitar star at Leeds Fest
With King Arthur on a quest
Climbing up Mount Everest
Sleeping in an eagle's nest
Stealing Blackbeard's treasure chest
And none of this is said in jest
All my mates are dead impressed.

Sticking to his words like glue
Knowing none of it is true
They just like the tale or two
Dad spins around his barbecue.

David Harmer

My Dad's Book

Tonight at our house it's pirates' night
Not silly costumes with scratchy beards
Rubber swords and a blow-up parrot
No, I mean the real thing.

Dad appears with the ancient book
It's covered in signs and silver stars
Creaking and dusty in battered green leather
He opens it up and it starts to glow.

We sit in the circle and Dad says the words
We shiver and tingle, the air grows warmer
Suddenly thick slices of moonbeams
Stream through the window, solid as stairs.

Up we climb, real pirates
There is our ship anchored in clouds
And away we sail on another adventure
Until the morning flies us home.

Yesterday we cleaned up Dodge City
The day before we flew to Saturn
Last week I scored the Cup Final winner
Mum and Dad danced in a famous film.

You can join us, all you need
Is the ancient book with the right words
I'll see you out there, dancing through moonlight
Until the morning flies us home.

David Harmer

Explorers

Let's explore the great outdoors,
Dad said, and leave our home behind.
Outside there's a wonderful world
and who knows what we'll find.

Let's wander about on mountains,
let's sleep beside the sea.
Let's disappear into deserts
and drift wherever we please.

Let's fish for tarpon off Florida
and watch the gulls screech by.
Let's trek between rainforest trees,
where we'll barely glimpse the sky.

We'll carry our home on our backs,
we'll camp by rivers and streams.
By day we'll follow railroad tracks,
by night we'll follow our dreams.

And we won't take the easy option,
we'll laugh when the going gets hard.
But just for tonight, we'll both play safe
and camp in our backyard.

Brian Moses

My Dad

My dad's bigger than your dad
He's as huge as a grizzly bear
His hands are like cranes
And his head has two brains
And he's totally covered in hair

My dad's smarter than your dad
Though he never tries to impress
He can spell long words
And recite French verbs
And he always wins Scrabble and chess

My dad's tougher than your dad
He has climbed to the top of K2
And he lived on bugs
And giant sea slugs
For a year in a cave in Peru

My dad's kinder than your dad
He'll help if you're down or depressed
And he always finds time
To read us a rhyme
Or give Mum a hug when she's stressed

Roger Stevens

The Go-kart

Dad built it with two old pram wheels,
One pushchair wheel and one tricycle wheel

Plus one wooden box – with optional old cushion,
Two planks of four by two, three feet of bailer twine
And numerous assorted nails, screws, nuts and bolts.

One Wednesday night and one Thursday night
And he had it finished.
Like God on the seventh day he looked at it
And said that it was good.

He was right too.
Friday night I painted it.
Odds and sods and leftovers from the shed,
Blue and black stripes, white stars, red dots.

Couldn't wait for it to dry.
Saturday afternoon – maiden voyage
Just me and dad
At the top of the orchard slope

Frighteningly fast
Perilously precarious
Boneshakingly brilliant
Went like the wind

The best ever,
The eventual envy of all my mates
Prized possession, I always loved the go-kart,
The go-kart that Dad built.

Paul Cookson

M for Mum

She's Magnetic
And Magnificent
Magnanimous, not Meek
A Muggle who is Magical
A Madonna with Mystique
She's a Melody that's Meaningful
The Most Majestic kind
Mazurka-like, a Minuet
She's Music in the Mind
Mellifluous, Mercurial
Memorable and Merry
She's every M for Marvellous
Found in the dictionary

Roger Stevens

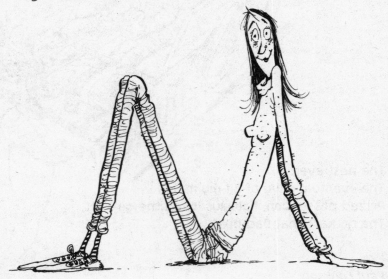

DaD's Pants

Dad's pants are big and baggy
Dad's pants are all antiques
Dad's pants are frayed and faded
Dad wears his pants for weeks

Dad's pants are so embarrassing
Dad's pants give us a fright
And when they're on the washing line
They block out all the light

Paul Cookson

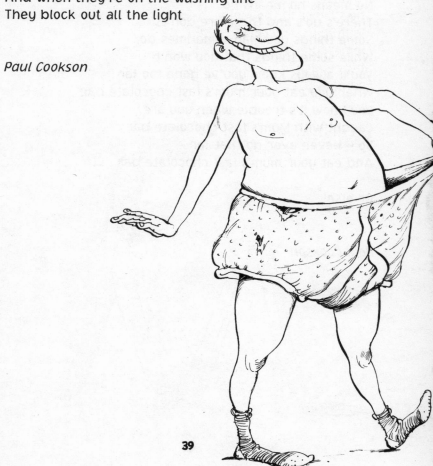

When Too Far Is Too Far

Limits are important and every child should know
What the boundaries are and how far you can go
Rules are rules are rules, be careful not to break them
Liberties are liberties so never try and take them

No means no means no
There's do's and there are don'ts
Some things you may sometimes do,
While some things that you won't
You'll always know you've gone too far
When you eat your mum's last chocolate bar
You know it's trouble when you are
Caught with Mum's last chocolate bar
So – never, ever go that far –
And eat your mum's last chocolate bar . . .

Or else!

Paul Cookson

CSI Dad's Shirt

You don't have to be a scientist
Of the forensic kind
To see what Dad's had for his tea
Look on his shirt and you will find

Blobs of egg yolk, baked-bean juice,
Chocolate, egg fried rice and cheese,
Curry, ketchup, butter, jam,
Crisp crumbs, beer and mushy peas

His shirt is three-dimensional
An Ordnance Survey map
Dad's leftovers all displayed
Upon his chest and lap

Paul Cookson

When I Grow UP

When I grow up
Will I have to wear
Old stripy woollen jumpers
Rescued from the dog basket?

When I grow up
Will I have to wear
Sandals with grey socks
And jeans that ride up
Under my arms?

When I grow up
Will I have to wear a T-shirt
That says
The Jesse Sands
Piano Accordion Band
World Tour 1998?

When I grow up
Will I have to dress
Like Dad?

Roger Stevens

Lovey-Dovey

When Dad and Mum go all lovey-dovey
we just don't know where to look.
My sister says, 'Cut it out you two,'
while I stick my nose in a book.

Mum has this faraway look on her face
while Dad has a silly grin.
'Don't mind us, kids,' he says,
we just wish they'd pack it in.

Dad calls Mum 'Little Sugarplum'
and Mum says, 'You handsome brute.'
Dad laughs and says, 'Look at your mum,
don't you think that she's cute?

'I guess that's why I married her,
she's my truly wonderful one.'
Mum says he doesn't mean any of it
but she thinks he's a lot of fun.

I just can't stand all the kissing,
just who do they think they are?
I caught them once on our driveway
snogging in the back of our car!

I hate it when they're lovey-dovey
but I hate it more when they fight,
when faces redden and tempers flare
and sharp words cut through the night.

So I'd rather they kissed and cuddled
and joked about and laughed,
at least we can tell everything's OK
when Mum and Dad are daft.

Brian Moses

A Hot Time in the Supermarket

When my mum gave my dad
The juiciest, most romantic kiss
Right there in the supermarket

And worse
Began to quickstep him down the aisle
To their favourite tune

I couldn't believe it.
Everybody stared.
My cheeks began to burn.

In our basket
The hot chilli sauce sweated
Ice cream melted
Ten frozen fish fingers defrosted
The fizzy wine popped its cork
The tomato sauce went redder
The tinned salmon pinker
The cream of mushroom soup
Boiled over
And the chicken drumsticks
Beat out a tango.

I had to have
Three tins of pop from the cold shelf
Two ice lollies
And a big swig of natural spring water
Just to get over it.

David Harmer

When Mum's Away

It's strange when Mum's away for the night.

Dad says he can do
all sorts of things he never does
when she's around.

So after he's sworn us to secrecy
with pound coins dropped into our pockets . . .

he cooks himself something dreadfully unhealthy.
He slobs out in front of the TV.
He forgets to walk the dog.
He turns Jimi Hendrix to full volume
    and air-guitars it round the room
    till our neighbours bang on the wall.
He finds old clothes to wear
    that everyone thought he'd thrown out years ago.
    ('No point,' he says. 'They're still comfortable.')
He rings up his mates and natters for hours.
    (We thought it was only Mum who did that.)
And more, much more, we're sure.

Only the dog knows everything our dad does when
Mum's away . . .

And she's not telling either!

Brian Moses

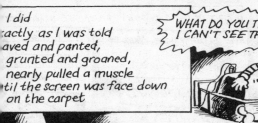

I did
exactly as I was told
waved and panted,
grunted and groaned,
nearly pulled a muscle
til the screen was face down
on the carpet

WHAT DO YOU THINK YOU ARE DOING? I CAN'T SEE THE FOOTBALL NOW!

I'm doing exactly as I was told turning the telly over!

Then I got shouted at
and sent to bed
It's not fair — parents tell you off
Even when you do
exactly as you are told

And they say daft things as well

Put the kettle on

Put the cat out

Why? Is it on fire?

Doesn't fit me — ooh it's hot, burned my head

Draw the curtains

OK — they're blue
with yellow flowers on

Come on —
we've got to catch the bus

It will be too heavy —
it will break my arms

Look at the time – it's getting late – run your bath

OK, bath – come on

If you have a runny nose, Mum says
Blow your nose
So I do – right in her face

WHAT ARE YOU DOING?

I'm doing exactly as I was told – I'm blowing my nose!

So they say

Don't be cheeky
watch your tongue

Less of your lip!

There – that's less of my lip

So Mum says –

I've had it up to here with you

Was it up to here before?

You drive me up the wall

Oh, we're up there are me and you in Spiderman's car?!

Do you want to go to bed without any tea?

Why, is it something nice like chips or pizza?

No, it's cabbage and broccoli

I'll go to bed now then

It's not fair – adults still tell us off
Even when we do
EXACTLY AS WE ARE TOLD!!!

Paul Cookson

Secrets

Dad keeps secrets from Mum.
Mum keeps secrets from Dad.

I wouldn't mind
but they both tell their secrets
to me . . .

I wish they'd keep them quiet,
I don't want to know about
Mum's unnecessary shopping,
a jumper, two skirts,
a somewhat extravagant party dress
and a handbag to replace the handbag
that Dad said was unnecessary
the last time she bought one.
(At least two weeks ago.)

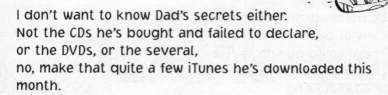

I don't want to know Dad's secrets either.
Not the CDs he's bought and failed to declare,
or the DVDs, or the several,
no, make that quite a few iTunes he's downloaded this
month.

Oh why do they tell me their secrets,
why don't they keep them to themselves?
I know one thing for sure . . .
MY secrets STAY secret!

Brian Moses

The Lazylympics

Dad's been watching the Olympics.

For the last two weeks we've seen him
take root on our settee,
watching our athletes
do amazing feats
on our TV.

'I'd like to be a medal winner,' he says.

So we thought maybe there could be
an Olympics for lazy people
like Dad.

There could be events like
floating on a lilo in the swimming pool
for the longest time,
or the most ring pulls ripped from
cans of beer.
There could be sports like
thinking about dog-walking
or lawnmowing,
or talking non-stop about football.

Dad would easily win a medal for yawning,
or eyebrow-raising, or taking a nap that lasts for
hours.

And we could be cheerleaders
cheering Dad on
as he slept his way to victory.

So many things our dad's good at,
it's just a shame they'll never have
a lazylympics
for sportsmen like Dad.

Brian Moses

Hello, Mum, I'm on the Bus

Hello, Mum.
Yes, I'm on the bus.
No, I'm fine.
I left my homework behind. Could you . . .
So could you . . .
Yes, I'm forgetful . . .
Yes, luckily it is screwed on.
Anyway, could you . . .
It's on my desk, next to . . .
I know I should have made my bed . . .
Yes, it is in a bit of a mess . . .
I know . . .
I was in a hurry because I overslept . . .
Yes, I should have gone to bed earlier
But I was doing my homework . . .
Anyway, about my homework . . .
Could you bring it to the . . .
OK, I'll tidy my room tonight. Mum?
Could you . . .
We're here now. I've got to get off.
I'm at the school.
About my homework . . . don't bother.
I'll say the dog ate it again.
Bye, Mum.

Roger Stevens

Marmite or Marmalade

Mum says, What would you like for breakfast?
And I say, *toast*.
Mum says,
What would you like on your toast?
And I say, *marmalade*.
Mum says,
We've run out of marmalade.
How about strawberry jam?
I say, *but I only like marmalade*.
We've got raspberry jam.
But I only like marmalade.
Blackcurrant jam? You like that.
Marmalade.
Marmite! You like that.
Marmalade.
Marmite.

Marmalade.
Marmite!
Marmalade!

Look, I can probably just scrape enough
marmalade from the bottom of the jar.
OK, I'll have Marmite then.
Look, there's just enough marmalade.
I'll have Marmite.
Marmalade.

Marmite.

Marmalade.

Marmite.

Marmalade.

Marmite!

Marmalade!

Have we got any cornflakes?

Roger Stevens

You'll Look Like One

'If you eat any more lollies
you'll start to look like one,'
Mum says.

'Well, what about you
and your cups of tea,
the same goes for you
as it does for me!'

I picture my Mum
as a huge mug of tea
and me a three-flavoured
drink on a stick.

'What's more,' she says,
'Don't make that face.
The wind will change
and leave you stuck!'

Knowing my luck
that's probably true!

I fix my face in
a fresh grimace,
the mug of tea wobbles
then smiles:

'Be off with you,'
she says,
and like a lolly
I melt away!

Brian Moses

AtChoo Haiku

Haiku . . . ha – haiku!

Dad is talking poetry

Each time he sneezes

Paul Cookson

Dad the Human BeatBox

The tuneless tunes he whistles
The knuckles he crick-cracks
The smacking of his lips
The teeth that he click-clacks

The squeaking of his fingers
As they burrow down his ear
The liquid grating rasp
As his throat begins to clear

The tocking of his tongue
The slapping on his thighs
The awful little creaking
When he rubs his eyes

The rhythm of his fingernails
On tables that he drums
The clicking and the snapping
Of his fingers and his thumbs

He sounds just like a horse
When he puffs his cheeks and blows
The snorting and the squelching
And the snuffling of his nose

There's never ever silence
When Dad is in the room
My dad the human beatbox
And we dance to his tune

Paul Cookson

Dad, Don't Dance

Whatever you do, don't dance, Dad
Whatever you do, don't dance
Don't wave your arms
Like a crazy buffoon
Displaying your charms
By the light of the moon
Trying to romance
A lady baboon
Whatever you do, don't dance.

When you try to dance
Your left leg retreats
And your right leg starts to advance
Whatever you do, don't dance, Dad
Has a ferret crawled into your pants?
Or maybe a hill full of ants
Don't samba
Don't rumba
You'll tumble
And stumble
Whatever you do, don't dance.

Don't glide up the aisle with a trolley
Or twirl the girl on the till
You've been banned from dancing in Tesco
Cos your tango made everyone ill

Whatever you do, don't dance, Dad
Whatever you do, don't dance
Don't make that weird face
Like you ate a sour plum
Don't waggle your hips
And stick out your bum
But most of all – PLEASE –
Don't smooch with Mum!
Whatever the circumstance
Whatever you do –
Dad, don't dance.

Roger Stevens

A Dad Remote Control

Our mum's got a dad remote control
that she points in his direction
whenever he slumps down on the settee
or starts to raise an objection.

She presses one button for 'walk the dog'
another for 'cook the tea'
and when she feels a little low
there's one labelled 'pamper me'.

Then there's 'run my bath' and 'pour my drink'
and 'time to stop lounging about'.
She presses a button for 'go and wash up'
and then 'take the rubbish out'.

And when she feels he should pay her attention
she operates 'please adore me'.
But when he goes on about football scores
she switches him off with 'you bore me'.

But when our mum goes out with her friends
and at last it's Dad's turn to choose
he points the remote control at himself
and presses the button marked 'snooze'.

Brian Moses

With a Dad Like This, Who Needs Enemies?

A dad with shorts
As baggy and wrinkled as an elephant's skin
Parading his pink and hairy knees all summer
Who does Tom Jones impressions
In the middle of a crowded street
Just as I walk past him with my friends.

A dad who all of a sudden
Very loudly walks and talks like a mad robot
In the checkout queue at the supermarket
And who makes mysterious whoopee-cushion noises
Every time he runs upstairs.

A dad who jokes about the clothes I wear
And who hates all my music, who argues
With my teacher, the woman at the garage
Shop assistants and the boy at the burger bar
Because French fries aren't proper chips.

A dad who pulls faces at me
When I'm on the school bus and who talks
In silly voices to all my friends, the kind of dad
Everyone thinks is great
But nobody else has to live with him
They don't know how tough that is!

David Harmer

Introducing Dad

If I may, Miss
I'd like to introduce my dad
Mum left us last year
And that made him really sad
He told me you were pretty
And his favourite colour's beige
And it isn't that uncommon
To date women half your age
And we all know that he's bald
Beneath that funny flick of hair
You just have to humour him
And pretend his hair's all there
His feet smell a bit funny
And his brain's a trifle slow
And you haven't got a boyfriend, Miss
So . . . could you please give Dad a go?

Roger Stevens

How Can I Be Lonely?

We're a family of eleven
And nearly everyone wants to play
So how can I possibly be lonely?
I ask myself each day

Mum works in the City of London
And Dad is a football scout
But that still leaves eight (not counting me)
So there's always someone about

Our cats, Alpha and Beta
They like a bit of fun
Chasing birds in the straggly bean patch
Or shadows in the sun

And our goldfish, Zap and Trevor
You'll never meet fish nicer
I can watch them swim round and round for hours
First one way then verse vicer

Harry the hamster's quite funny
With his death-defying tricks
And Judy, our dog, doesn't say very much
But she's brilliant at bringing back sticks

You can chat with Peter the budgie
He'll discuss football, the Villa or Man U
He can talk the hind legs off a python
He can talk till his face turns blue

We're a family of eleven
And nearly everyone wants to play
So how can I possibly be lonely?
I ask myself each day

Oh, I nearly forgot – that's only ten
I've not mentioned my very best mate
If ever, by chance, I do get lonely
I chat to the garden gate

Roger Stevens

Granny Said a
Wise Thing

Granny said a wise thing
when we were quite young.
Granny, that's my mum's mum,
lived across town, half a mile away,
unlike Dad's mum, who lived next door
in a house called Bleak House,
named after Charles Dickens's book,
the writer who wrote *Oliver*,
which became a musical –
remember, we saw it at the village hall
but the piano was out of tune
and has been since Mr Dupree died
and Mr Dupree wasn't French like everyone thought
but was born in Doddington
but he *was* blind
and was never captured by aliens
and taken on a tour of the universe,
he just made that up,
like he made up his name,
anyway, as Granny once
    said, very wisely . . .
Now what did she say?
    I've forgotten.

Roger Stevens

And always
remember . . .

Watch Out, Our Granny's About!

When Granny took up kick-boxing
We said, 'Well, that won't last.'
But we've never seen her move
So lightly or so fast.
She whirls and twirls, leaps about
Throws snap kicks in the air.
You want to tell her she's too old
You can try it – if you dare.

David Harmer

HAH!

Great-gran Is Manic on Her Motorbike

Shout out loud, say what you like
Great-gran is manic on her motorbike!

Last week her helmet touched the stars
when she zoomed over thirty cars
she didn't quibble, didn't fuss
when they added a double-decker bus.

Shout out loud, say what you like
Great-gran is manic on her motorbike!

She's a headline-hunting, bike-stunting
wacky, wild one-woman show
she revs and roars to wild applause
there is no place her bike won't go
she gives them shivers jumping rivers
and balancing across high wires
with a cheer she changes gear
flies her bike through blazing tyres.

Shout out loud, say what you like
Great-gran is manic on her motorbike!

She told me when she quits bike riding
she's going to take up paragliding
I'll always be her greatest fan
my dazzling, daredevil, manic Great-gran!

Shout out loud, say what you like
Great-gran is manic on her motorbike!

David Harmer

We're Glad to Be Rid of Madrid

When Dad first said 'Spain' we thought 'Wow!'
We thought sand and sea and sun,
we thought Benidorm or Minorca
with discos, parties and fun.
Not monuments and museums
and trailing round a city
but Dad said this was culture,
we were seeing the real nitty-gritty.

So he flapped around with the guidebook,
reading out pages from history,
the wars, the struggles, the heroes,
no clearer now, still a mystery.
'This is it,' Dad would say as he waved an arm,
'Just look at the beauty, the grace,
the charm of all this architecture,
it's a truly amazing place.'

It could have been amazing for us
if we'd seen the football teams
Real Madrid or Atlético,
now they're the stuff of our dreams.
A tour round their footy grounds
would have helped to ease our pain,
but Dad said, 'No way, José,'
that wasn't why we'd come to Spain.

So off we'd go yet again
to another historical site

and we'd rush across a plaza
or nip through a parque at night.
We'd see sculptures in a museo
and the palace of a Spanish king
till the final day and Dad had to admit
we'd seen almost everything.

But for us it had been a blur,
all those city sights that we passed,
and now that we're back on the plane
it's, 'Adios, Madrid,' at last.
'Adios, Madrid, and good riddance,'
we're glad that the holiday's through
and next year, Dad, if you mention Spain,
it's, 'No way, José,' to you too!

Brian Moses

NB: José is
pronounced
'Ho-ZAY'

EL SID

Getting Really Good Now

Once we thought we could change things,
we really thought we could,
if they argued over us
then we could be extra good.
But it never seemed to work
even if we weren't to blame,
it did no good at all,
they argued just the same.

But we're getting really good now
at keeping out of the way.

Why, oh why do they do it?
Why do our parents fight?
We hear them arguing downstairs
while we're in bed at night.
Sometimes it's just sniping,
other times it's open war.
Why, oh why do they do it?
What are they fighting for?

But we're getting really good now
at keeping out of the way.

We've learned to keep our heads down,
to stay clear of the flak,
we've learned all kinds of tricks
like covering our backs.
And however much they argue,
the hurtful things they say,
we're both in this together
just getting through each day.

But we're getting really good now
at keeping out of the way.

Brian Moses

Every Year

Every year it's the same,
we're packing our car in the rain,
heaving cases on to the roof
(good training for weightlifters
    or scene-shifters).
And then when we get to the campsite,
we're pitching our tent
on a patch of ground
that's halfway between a swamp and a lake,
while Mum's in the back of the car
with the Primus, trying to make some tea.
And Dad and I are lashing things down
while the wind full bellies our tent.
And we're held in the teeth of a gale
till one by one we hammer the stakes
and the tent, like an angry animal,
loses its strength and settles down.

And each year we say
never again.
And each year we say
we'll jet off to Spain
but we don't.

Brian Moses

The Things They Say!

My dad says
He's as old as the moon
With a face made of cheese
And marbles for eyes.

My mum says
She's really a lioness
Prowling the night
Queen of the cats.

My dad says
He's really a rock star
And his best friend
Is the King of Peru.

My mum says
She's often an astronaut
Spends every Tuesday
Flying to Mars.

What I say is
They are both bonkers!
The best mum and dad
In the whole world.

David Harmer

They Pinch Your Prezzies If They Can!

Christmas night
Snuggled down, waiting for Santa
Snow splodging the silent windows
I drift asleep.

Until
I hear a whoop, a shout, a yell
The buzzing of engines
The crashing of cars
The angry whine of burning brakes
Screeching round corners.

I creep downstairs
The clamour increases
There they are! What a cheek!
Mum and Dad on my new console
The one they said I'd get for Christmas.

They're powering the street of LA
After dark in pulsating hot rods
Slamming and snarling into the night.
Dad is yelling, 'Yo! I'm winning!'
Mum is yelling, 'No way, you loser!'
They don't even know I'm there!

I sneak back to bed
Hoping they won't break my new game
They'd better stop soon
Go to sleep like everyone else,
Snuggled down, waiting for Santa.

David Harmer

My Dad the Sumo Wrestler

My dad and me
play at sumo wrestling.

He squats on his haunches
pushes out his big stomach
(which isn't that hard as he's got three)

sticks out his tongue
yells, then twists
his face into a distorted mask

(I mean an expression
slightly less ugly than he is already!)

I'm the other side of the room
and I do the same.

We grunt and stomp
towards each other in slow motion
our tummies collide
like two giant balloons exploding.

We start to grapple
and I always win
because I tickle him
really hard.

He falls over laughing
lands in a heap of gurgling giggles

and I bounce up and down on his back
in celebration.

David Harmer

The Best Way for Mum to Spend Mother's Day

I've sent Billy our boxer dog
to the shops for the paper.

I've sent Danny, our eldest
to the supermarket.

I've sent Jenny, our youngest
to cook dinner for Granny.

I've sent Franny, the middle one
off to town for some sweets.

I've sent Bernie our budgie
on a long flight to Scunthorpe.

I've sent Benny, my husband
off to football.

I've sent Jimmy our guinea pig
for a roll in his ball.

I've sent Herbie our hamster
to sleep for a month.

I'm lying here in bed
drinking my tea.

Eating my choccies
opening my prezzies.

And I'm going to stay here
all day!

David Harmer

Dad's Hat-trick Celebrations

When Dad scored a goal in the garden
He celebrated with glee
He put his T-shirt over his head
And ran into a tree!

So when he scored his second
He should have had more sense
He tried to slide but couldn't stop
And smashed the garden fence!

His hat-trick handstand antics tried
To claim the ball and grab it
He slipped and tripped, his trousers ripped
And he flattened next door's rabbit!

When Mum came out and shouted
It was me he blamed
But luckily I'd filmed it
Now it's been on *You've Been Framed*!

Paul Cookson